MW01268281

[SURVIVING] THE IMPOSSIBLE

SURVIVING
THE YELLOWSTONE
SUPERVOLCANO

CHARLIE OGDEN

Gareth Stevens
PUBLISHING

Please visit our website, **www.garethstevens.com**.
For a free color catalog of all our high-quality books,
call toll free 1-800-542-2595 or fax 1-877-542-2596.

CATALOGING-IN-PUBLICATION DATA

Names: Ogden, Charlie.
Title: Surviving the Yellowstone supervolcano / Charlie Ogden.
Description: New York : Gareth Stevens Publishing, 2018. | Series: Surviving the impossible | Includes index.
Identifiers: ISBN 9781538214558 (pbk.) | ISBN 9781538214268 (library bound) | ISBN 9781538214565 (6 pack)
Subjects: LCSH: Volcanoes--Juvenile literature. | Yellowstone National Park -- Juvenile literature. |
  Disasters--Juvenile literature. | Survival--Juvenile literature.
Classification: LCC QE521.3 O43 2018 | DDC 551.21--dc23

Published in 2018 by
Gareth Stevens Publishing
111 East 14th Street, Suite 349
New York, NY 10003

Copyright © 2018 BookLife

Written by: Charlie Ogden
Edited by: Kirsty Holmes
Designed by: Matt Rumbelow

Photo credits: Abbreviations: l-left, r-right, b-bottom, t-top, c-center, m-middle. Images are courtesy of Shutterstock.com. With thanks to Getty Images, Thinkstock Photo and iStockphoto. Cover: bg – , 2 – Ammit Jack, 4t – Wead, 4b – BlackMac, 5 – solarseven, 6 – PFMphotostock, 7 – Wisanu Boonrawd, 8t – Andrea Danti, 8b – lava mix, 9 – Skreidzeleu, 10 – austinding, 11bg – Catmando, 11b – Tatiana Popova, 12 – sdecoret, 13 – VarnaK, 14bg – Nickolad Warner, 14b – Ratthaphong Ekariyasap, 14t – Pavel Hlystov, 15 – Ruslan Shaforostov, 16t – photobac, 16b – Max-Studio, 17t – xshot, 17b – Patrizio Martorana, 18t – supersaiyan3, 18b – Volodymyr Krasyuk, 19 – Iosonsky, 20t – Vladislav S, 20b – Photovolcanica.com, 21 – Wead, 22t – Dudarev Mikhail, 22b – Dewi Putra, 23 – Stokkete, 24 – Byelikova Oksana, 25t – Audy39, 25b – Africa Studio, 26 – BT Image, 27 – Marvin Minder, 28 – Wojciech Dziadosz, 29 – GrAl, 30 – Alexander Piragis

All rights reserved. No part of this book may be reproduced in any
form without permission from the publisher, except by a reviewer.

Printed in the United States of America
CPSIA compliance information: Batch CW18GS. For further information contact
Gareth Stevens, New York, New York at 1-800-542-2595.

CONTENTS

PAGE 4 Extreme Eruptions

Page 6 Superpowered Supervolcanoes

Page 8 The Science Behind Supervolcances

Page 10 Warning: Danger!

Page 12 Take Cover

Page 16 Emergency Survival Supplies

Page 20 Go with the Pyroclastic Flow

Page 26 Natural Disasters

Page 28 Climate Change

Page 30 Surviving the Yellowstone Supervolcano

Page 31 Glossary

Page 32 Index

Words that look like THIS can be found in the glossary on page 31.

EXTREME ERUPTIONS

Imagine a force so mind-bendingly powerful that it could plunge the entire world into darkness, change the weather all over the globe, and kill hundreds of thousands of people in just one day. You might ask yourself, who or what could do this? Aliens? Robots? Mega-sized meteorites? Well, no, actually. It's the supersized eruption of a supervolcano.

Need to move...

POWERLESS IN POMPEII

Look back in time about 2,000 years ago to the ancient Roman city of Pompeii, in Italy. A thunderous roar filled the sky as rocks, ash, and gas shot up into the air. Mount Vesuvius, the nearby volcano, erupted with great force. The unlucky few thousand people who were in Pompeii at the time were instantly killed as the volcano filled the sky with superheated air, shook the ground, and buried the whole city in a grimy layer of volcanic ash.

FIRE BURN AND CAULDRON BUBBLE

The unstoppable force of a volcanic eruption – able to destroy towns, cities, and humans alike – has always been a mystery to humans. Some ancient cultures in South America believed that volcanoes were linked to the gods. They even made human sacrifices to keep the gods happy. Pretty scary, right? Other peoples, including the Romans, believed that some volcanoes were an entrance to the underworld, with their fiery pits of doom.

SUPERPOWERED SUPERVOLCANOES

These living, breathing fire monsters have fascinated and terrified us in equal measure for thousands of years. But what happens when our fears become reality and a supersized eruption is right on our doorstep?

SLEEPING GIANTS

Vesuvius was just a regular-sized volcano. So imagine the effects of an eruption from a volcano at least 1,000 times that size. Well, a supervolcano is just that. It's basically a massive volcano that can unleash CATASTROPHIC damage in one awe-inspiring mega-blast. But don't worry too much. Experts think that they only erupt every million years or so. One thing is for sure – when one erupts, you'll know about it!

One of the largest and most feared supervolcanoes in the world – the Yellowstone supervolcano in the United States – is expected to erupt soon. Although, in supervolcano-speak, soon could mean next month, in the next 25 years, or the next 250,000 years.

Even now, volcano experts don't know enough about these fiery giants to predict their eruptions. While we don't know exactly when Yellowstone is going to erupt, we do know that it definitely will. When it does, you're going to need to know how to escape it alive.

7

THE SCIENCE BEHIND SUPERVOLCANOES

This little planet that we live on may look solid and stable, but it's really made up of a number of huge plates of rock called tectonic plates. These plates are always moving, colliding, and sliding against each other. This is what creates earthquakes and the **PRESSURE ZONES** that can cause volcanic eruptions.

Bit too warm

TURNING UP THE PRESSURE

Underneath the moving and colliding plates is scorching-hot melted rock called magma. Magma sometimes collects in high pressure areas called magma chambers beneath the Earth's **CRUST**. When the pressure in a magma chamber builds and builds over hundreds, thousands, or millions of years, it can cause the magma to be pushed upwards, out of the Earth's crust in one supercharged explosion. This is a volcanic eruption.

YELLOWSTONE'S FURY

Yellowstone has enough magma in it's magma chamber and in the magmal RESERVOIR below to fill the Grand Canyon 14 times over. That's a LOT of deadly, sizzling rock. Once the pressure in the magma chamber builds to unbearable levels, white-hot magma will force itself through the Earth's crust as lava. This, along with gases, ash, and red-hot pieces of rock will shoot up to 19 miles (30 km) into the air.

It's not just the lava that you've got to deal with – volcanic eruptions can cause a whole world of deadly natural disasters, including LANDSLIDES and AVALANCHES.

So, what can you do? Well, for a start, try to avoid living too close to any active volcanoes, especially a supervolcano. The further away you are from an eruption, the more chance you have of surviving it.

9

WARNING: DANGER!

SHAKE, RATTLE AND ROLL

It's pretty much impossible to tell exactly when the next Yellowstone supervolcano mega-blast will happen. But don't worry. Before the actual eruption happens, there will be signs to watch out for that will hopefully warn you of your impending doom.

For months leading up to the mega-blast, you might notice an increased number of earthquakes. There will usually be lots of them in the same area at the same time. These are called earthquake swarms. Earthquakes can be a sign of perfectly normal supervolcanic activity, or a sign that a catastrophic, life-changing disaster is heading your way. Either way, you'll need to be prepared.

NEWS FLASH!

You might turn on the TV one day to watch your favorite show. You could be sitting comfortably as the opening theme song starts to play when suddenly, it's interrupted by a newsflash: "The Yellowstone supervolcano is predicted to erupt in the next 24 hours!" You feel the blood pumping around your body and beads of sweat roll down your forehead as you realize the thing that you've been dreading is finally happening – the Yellowstone supervolcano is about to erupt.

Take a few deep breaths and calm down. You'll need to keep a clear head if you want to survive.

TAKE COVER

f you want to survive the mega-blast, you're going
to need to keep your cool, forget your fears, and
focus your energy on trying to survive the blast of
gas, rock, and DEBRIS that's coming your way.
Take your babbling siblings, hysterical parents, and
anyone else you might want to keep around and
head out of the danger zone.

EVACUATE, EVACUATE!

If you're looking to survive a supervolcano eruption, timing is everything. If you're really lucky, you might find out about the eruption days or even weeks before it happens. If this is the case, evacuate the danger zone as soon as possible. The most dangerous area is called the pyroclastic zone, and it includes everything within about 50 miles (80 km) from the blast. After the eruption, scorching-hot gas and ash will most likely destroy everything in this zone, so try to avoid it if you want to survive.

Now's the time to take that much-needed break to a faraway island. Yellowstone's eruption is expected to affect most areas of North America immediately by **CONTAMINATING** water and crops. Transportation will be halted and communication will be stopped as everything becomes buried under the ash.

The farther away you are from Yellowstone the better. It doesn't matter if it is Madagascar, Australia, or outer space — just start heading in the opposite direction. The moon is probably a safe bet!

THINK FAST, ACT QUICK

If you don't have the luxury of having weeks to prepare for the mega-blast, then run for cover — and quickly! Without a decent place to hide, you don't have a chance of surviving the Yellowstone supervolcano eruption. If you can, get indoors. Find a strong building, then head upstairs — the higher the better!

NOWHERE TO RUN, NOWHERE TO HIDE

If you can't find shelter, then get to higher ground. Landslides and flooding are all highly likely after a massive eruption. All of these can be deadly in low-lying areas such as valleys and rivers, which are likely to flood first. So, if you're not washed away by water and mud, get to high ground and stay there until the danger has passed.

Try to protect yourself from flying debris and scorching-hot rocks by staying below the of hills if possible.

Hiding behind trees won't help you here – you'll be flattened in seconds along with them. Also, try to pick a hiding place that's UPWIND of the volcano. When the gigantic cloud of gas and ash starts to head your way, you'll give yourself the best chance of survival if you're not directly in its path.

EMERGENCY SURVIVAL SUPPLIES

If you're going to survive the eruption, then you're going to need to gather enough supplies to tough this out for a while. The Yellowstone eruption could mean you're stuck inside one building for weeks or even months without food, clean water, or communication with the outside world. Remember, only take the essentials for your survival – your favorite pair of shoes won't be much use to you as scorching-hot gas flows towards you.

FOOD

You definitely can't run out to the store to buy your favorite cereal, soda, or cookies, so you're going to need to plan ahead. Focus on STOCKPILING canned foods like beans, sweet corn, and spaghetti noodles, which can last for a number of years. Make sure you have enough food to last you for at least a couple of months. You don't want to starve to death, or consider eating your annoying little brother or sister...

WATER, WATER EVERYWHERE, BUT NOT A DROP TO DRINK

Avoid drinking tap water, or any water from freshwater sources. The huge amount of falling ash is likely to contaminate freshwater sources for hundreds of miles around the blast. Remember to only drink bottled water and make sure you've got enough to last you. When the authorities say it's safe, you can get back to lapping up water from the tap, a river, or even your dog's water bowl.

MARVELOUS MEDICINE

Medical supplies are essential to making sure that you survive the toughest time of your life. If you survive the mega-blast and any number of the catastrophic natural disasters that will follow, then you'd be pretty annoyed if a bad bout of flu finally gets you. Make sure you take along a first aid kit complete with essential medicines and a few bandages.

IS THERE ANYBODY OUT THERE?

Prepare to be cut off completely from the outside world. After the mega-blast, power lines will be destroyed, and so will all lines of communication that rely on electricity, including phones, televisions, and laptops. Take a battery-powered radio and plenty of extra batteries with you. This might be the only way the outside world can reach you, if at all.

LET THERE BE LIGHT

If the power's out, you'll have no way of finding the bathroom, knowing what canned food you're eating, or who's poking their bony elbow into your back in the night. You can't even rely on sunlight in the daytime, because the amount of ash released during the eruption will block out the sun and plunge you into darkness. Avoid these situations by taking a battery-powered flashlight and plenty of extra batteries so you can see what you and everyone else is doing at all times.

Hopefully you'll have your family to comfort you. But if not, don't worry. Find other survivors and make friends with them until you can find your friends and family.

GO WITH THE PYROCLASTIC FLOW

Pyroclastic flows are one of the first – and scariest – things that you're going to face after an eruption. The eruption will shoot rocks, PUMICE, ash, and volcanic gas into the air, which will collect in a scorching-hot mushroom-like cloud. This is a pyroclastic flow. Pyroclastic flows can scorch and destroy everything in their paths – whole forests have been flattened, buildings shattered, and farmlands scorched by these unforgiving beasts.

CLOUDY WITH A CHANCE OF ROCK BALLS

Scorching-hot pieces of rock, ranging in size from fine, dust-like particles to huge boulders, will be picked up in the pyroclastic flow and will eventually be dropped somewhere else. This is particularly bad news if you're stuck outside without protection. First, try to protect yourself by hiding below natural barriers. Second, crouch down on the ground, facing away from the volcano and protect your head with a backpack or your arms. These small but essential measures could stop you from being instantly killed or seriously burnt.

IF YOU CAN'T HANDLE THE HEAT . . .

Heat is going to be your biggest enemy if you happen to be stuck in the middle of a pyroclastic flow. Pyroclastic flows can scorch and burn your skin and lungs with extreme temperatures of over 752 °F (400 °C). If you survive the pyroclastic flow, it might be with some serious life-threatening burns. Treat these as soon as possible. If you or any family members are burnt, remove any clothing that isn't stuck to the burns, cover the burn in a layer of gauze and give them medicine for the pain.

IT'S RAINING ASH

The ash that will fall from the pyroclastic flow will fall for hundreds of miles from the original blast. The ash will block out the sun from the sky and contaminate our water sources and the air that we breathe. To survive, you need to keep this ash out of your home so that you don't breathe too much of it in.

HOMES

To protect your hideout, you need to make sure there is no way for the ash to get in. Close and lock all windows and doors, and cover any remaining gaps with damp towels to stop absolutely anything from entering. Turn off your air conditioning system if you have one, as it will bring in contaminated air from the outside. If possible, try to avoid going outside until the authorities tell you it's safe.

PROTECTION

If you do have to go outside, you need to be well protected. To protect your skin from irritation, wear a long-sleeved shirt and pants. Don't forget some airtight goggles to protect your eyes. To avoid ash getting into your lungs, which could seriously hurt or even kill you, you'll need to buy an air-purifying respirator. These handy devices will filter out the ash from the air, so the air you breathe in is clean. If you haven't got one of these handy gadgets, make sure you cover your nose and mouth with a damp cloth when you go outside.

Wear your goggles and air-purifying respirator at all times. Even if you think that your hideout is ash free, it has a funny way of creeping in through even the smallest of gaps.

LIFE'S A GAS

If red-hot rocks and ash weren't enough to deal with, the volcanic gases released during an eruption can cause you some series problems too. The supervolcano will spew out a number of mostly harmless gases, but some of them, like carbon dioxide and hydrogen sulphide, can be deadly.

CARBON DIOXIDE

Carbon dioxide – or CO_2 – currently exists in the air in small amounts, but when too much spews out of a supervolcano, it can become deadly. It's colorless, ODORLESS, and almost impossible to detect. Low-lying areas will turn into CO_2 traps after the eruption, so avoiding these areas could just save your life.

HYDROGEN SULPHIDE

Hydrogen sulphide is a colorless, FLAMMABLE gas that smells like the rotten egg sandwiches that have been sweating away in your lunch box all day. The best tool you have to detect the presence of this stinky gas is your nose. Exposure to large amounts of hydrogen sulphide can cause you to fall unconscious in less than five minutes and die within an hour.

NATURAL DISASTERS

If you've managed to survive both the mega-blast and the pyroclastic flow, then you've got to look ahead to the next challenges you're going to face. The extreme temperatures contained within the pyroclastic flow can start a whole chain of events that can lead to deadly natural disasters all over the globe. Just what you needed, right?

LAHARS AND LANDSLIDES

Lahars and landslides are common after volcanic eruptions. A lahar is a type of mudflow that consists of a mixture of water and rock. It can travel at speeds of more than 124 miles (200 km) an hour. They look like extremely fast-flowing rivers of concrete and they swallow everything in their path, including soil, buildings, and even bridges, as they rush downstream. Landslides are massive quantities of rock and soil that slide or fall downwards. If landslides pick up enough water on the way, they can easily turn into lahars too.

If you're caught up in a lahar or a landslide, the most important thing you need to do is get to higher ground or the highest floor of your house. Avoid low-lying areas like valleys and riverbanks. If you have little or no warning of a landslide or a lahar, try to move out of its path as quickly as possible. If escape isn't possible, curl into a tight ball and try to protect your head with your hands or a helmet if you have one.

27

CLIMATE CHANGE

If you've managed to make it through all these natural disasters, then you deserve a break. But don't rest up for too long. You've still got to deal with the long-term effects of a supervolcanic eruption. The eruption of Yellowstone would change the weather of the entire world for many, many years to come.

ICE COOL

When they erupt, volcanoes release a gas called sulfur dioxide into the ATMOSPHERE. Scientists believe that this causes the CLIMATE to cool after a supervolcanic eruption. The eruption of Yellowstone is expected to release massive amounts of sulfur, which would take just three weeks to travel around the whole planet. This would cause global temperatures to drop by up to 53 °F (12 °C) for up to ten years. The colder temperatures could cause droughts – long periods without rain – and destroy crops, which could kill both humans and animals.

28

Because scientists know so little about what will actually happen when the climate becomes colder, it's difficult to predict exactly how to survive these times. The most important thing is to be prepared for what might be coming your way. Stock up on food, water, and warm clothes to survive the never-ending winter and be hopeful — you've survived much worse than this so far.

SURVIVING THE YELLOWSTONE SUPERVOLCANO

If you follow this guide, then you might just survive a Yellowstone supervolcano eruption. Remember, if you have time, always try to evacuate the danger zone. If you can't, you'll need to have a decent hideout that is well stocked with food, supplies, and essential medicines. Whatever the mega-blast has to throw at you – from scorching-hot boulders, superheated ash raining from the sky, poisonous gases, to lahars and landslides – just remember: you're ready for this.

If you manage to survive the impossible, then take some time to focus on the quiet life for a change. Do the things you like to do, and surround yourself with the people that you love. You've been through a lot, so take a break, enjoy your life, and rest assured you're unlikely to deal with another supervolcano eruption in your lifetime. But if you do, at least you'll know what to do.

GLOSSARY

ATMOSPHERE — the mixture of gases that make up the air and surround the Earth

AVALANCHES — large, often dangerous, masses of snow, ice, and rock that travel down mountains at high speeds

CATASTROPHIC — a disastrous event

CLIMATE — the common weather in a certain place

CONTAMINATING — to make something unclean by adding a poisonous or polluting substance to it

CRUST — the hard outer layer of the Earth

DEBRIS — the remains of anything that has been broken down or destroyed

FLAMMABLE — something that can be easily set on fire

LANDSLIDES — large amounts of earth and rock that fall down hillsides or mountains, often caused by heavy rain or earthquakes

ODORLESS — something that you can't smell

PRESSURE ZONES — areas where pressure builds up

PUMICE — a gray stone that comes from volcanoes

RESERVOIR — a natural chamber that holds liquid, such as magma

RIDGELINES — lines formed along the highest points of mountain ranges or hills

STOCKPILING — the act of saving a supply of materials

UPWIND — the opposite direction to the way the wind is blowing

INDEX

air 4, 9, 20-24

ash 4, 9, 13, 15, 17, 19-20, 22-24, 30

breathing 6, 11, 22-23

carbon dioxide 24

climate change 28-29

communication 13, 16, 18

crust 8-9

debris 12, 15

earthquake 8, 10

flows 16, 20-22, 26-27

food 16, 19, 29-30

gases 4, 9, 12-13, 15-16, 20, 24-25, 28, 30

heat 4, 21, 30

hideout 22-23, 30

hydrogen sulphide 24-25

lahars 27, 30

landslide 9, 15, 27, 30

lava 9

light 19

magma 8-9

magma chamber 8-9

medicine 18, 21, 30

Mount Vesuvius 4, 6

natural disasters 9, 18, 26, 28

news 11

Pompeii 4

pressure 8-9

pumice 20

pyroclastic 13, 20-22, 26

rock 4, 8-9, 12, 15, 20-21, 24, 27

shelter 15

supplies 16, 18, 30

tectonic plates 8

temperature 21, 26, 28

water 13, 15-17, 22, 27, 29

zones 8, 12-13, 30